NO TV?
NO FAIR!

NO TV?
NO FAIR!

by

Karin Adams

James Lorimer & Company Ltd., Publishers
Toronto

James Lorimer & Company Ltd. acknowledges the support of the
Ontario Arts Council. We acknowledge the support of the Government
of Canada through the Book Publishing Industry Development
Program (BPIDP) for our publishing activities. We acknowledge the
support of the Canada Council for the Arts for our publishing program.
We acknowledge the support of the Government of Ontario through
the Ontario Media Development Corporation's Ontario Book Initiative.

Cover design: Meredith Bangay

Library and Archives Canada Cataloguing in Publication

Adams, Karin

  No TV? no fair! / by Karin Adams.

ISBN 978-1-55277-471-7

  1. Television — Juvenile fiction. I. Title.

PS8601.D453N6 2010   jC813'.6   C2009-906658-0

James Lorimer & Company Ltd.,
Publishers
317 Adelaide Street West
Suite #1002
Toronto, Ontario, M5V 1P9
www.lorimer.ca

Distributed in the
United States by:
Orca Book Publishers
P.O. Box 468
Custer, WA U.S.A.
98240-0468

Printed and bound in Canada.
Manufactured by Webcom in Toronto, Ontario, Canada in February
2010. Job # 366637

For Gordon

1

The Rule

Zap!

Chloe Lambert's mom switched off the TV. Chloe scrunched up her face as she stared at the blank screen. She was in the middle of watching her all-time favourite show, *The Taylor Twins*. Jake and Josh Taylor were just about to perform their latest hit song, "Heartbreak Summer."

"We're shutting off the television for one month," Chloe's mom announced. "Starting *now*."

Chloe's face suddenly became unscrunched. Her eyes got very wide. Her mouth dropped open. No TV for a month? She was so surprised, she couldn't say a word. Her mom must be joking!

Chloe checked her mom's face. She wasn't joking.

Stomp. Stomp. STOMP!

Chloe's older brother Mark stormed down the two steps that led into the family room. *What's he doing here?* Chloe thought. Mark still had seventeen minutes left in his turn on the computer. She knew this because in *exactly* seventeen minutes, the computer was all hers. Mark slumped onto the couch beside her. His dark, messy hair hung in his eyes, but Chloe could still see the grouchy look on his face. Grouchier than usual, that is. Mark was thirteen and, according to Chloe's parents, suffered from "perma-frown."

Chloe's dad followed Mark into the family room and stood in front of the TV beside their mom. Chloe's parents were still in their work clothes. Her mom was dressed in a navy skirt and a white blouse, and her dark hair was pulled back. Her dad wore a grey shirt tucked into black dress pants, and had his glasses on. He usually only wore his glasses for work, and Chloe always thought they made him look serious. In fact, at that moment, both her parents looked like they meant business.

"We've made a family decision," Chloe's mom said. "No TV and no computer in our house for the next thirty days."

What? Chloe's mouth opened even wider. *No computer, either?* It was bad enough that Chloe had to live without *The Taylor Twins*, *My Two Crazy Lives*, and *Rock School*, just to name a few of her favourite shows. But they wanted her to give up her computer games, too?

"No fair!" grumbled Mark. "How is this a family decision? *I'm* part of the family, and this sure wasn't *my* decision."

"What about me?" Chloe said. "I wasn't even finished watching *The Taylor Twins*. And I was going to beat the last level of *Swamp Creature Showdown 2* on the computer today."

"Dumb game," Mark muttered through his perma-frown.

"No it's *not*," Chloe said. "Looking up hockey stats for an hour is dumb." She gave her brother a kick. A few of Chloe's light brown curls came loose from her pink hair band and tumbled into her face. "Plus, Sasha told me at school today that there's a brand new game on my all-time favourite website."

"Is it called *Dumb Baby Game 3*?" Mark asked, returning Chloe's kick.

"Mark!" said their dad, with a warning look on his face.

"No!" Chloe said, tossing her hair out of her eyes. "It's *Interstellar Jellyfish Invasion*. You have to shoot raspberry jam at alien jellyfish who are trying to take over the world."

"Sounds exciting," Mark said sarcastically.

"I was going to play it on the computer in . . ." Chloe checked the clock on the DVD player, "sixteen minutes!"

Their parents looked at each other and sighed.

"Listen, you guys," their dad said. "We're not saying that you can never watch TV or play computer games again. It's only for a month."

"How come?" Mark asked. "We didn't do anything wrong!"

10

"This isn't a punishment," their dad continued, reaching up to rub the bristly hairs on his shaved head. "It's more like . . . an experiment."

Some experiment! Chloe thought.

"Your dad and I had a serious discussion about all the time we spend with the TV and our computers," said their mom. "It's getting to be unhealthy."

Chloe did a quick calculation of her daily TV and computer time. Sure, she spent a couple of hours watching TV or playing the computer every day, but . . .

"I spend way more time at school!" Chloe argued. "Does that mean school is unhealthy, too?"

"Maybe we should try not going to school for a month," Mark said. "I like *that* experiment."

Their dad rolled his eyes. "Come on, guys. You know what we mean. Too much TV and computer is a waste of time. It's turning our brains into mush."

Chloe scowled. Her brain felt just fine, thank you very much!

"We're going to see what it feels like to go offline," their dad continued. "It might even be fun!"

Chloe crossed her arms tight across her chest. Mark shook his head.

"All winter we complain about the never-ending cold here in Winnipeg," their mom said. "It's almost June, and the weather is absolutely gorgeous. Think of all the things you can do when you aren't sitting inside, in front of a screen."

"You could be riding your bikes, playing basketball in the driveway, or having water fights," their dad suggested.

Chloe huffed. She didn't want to play outside. She wanted to fly a silver command vessel in outer space and shoot jam at alien jellyfish. And after that, she wanted to see if Maddie Mariposa on *My Two Crazy Lives* finally tells her mom that she's a world-famous fashion designer when she's not at school.

Suddenly, a horrible thought occurred to Chloe. "What about the season finale of *The*

Taylor Twins?" she said, her face full of distress. "It's on in two weeks. Can I at least watch that? Sasha says it's going to be HUGE!" Chloe's heart was pounding. Surely her parents would let her watch the season finale of her favourite show. They knew how much she loved it.

But her dad shook his head. "I'm sorry, Chloe, but we could always find an excuse not to go offline. The thirty days start right now."

Chloe stood up, fists clenched, and glared at her parents. How could they be so mean? This was so unfair! She felt her face get hot and red.

Then, even though Chloe was ten and in grade four, she knew she was going to do something she hadn't done since she was really, really small. She couldn't help it.

BOOM! Her foot came crashing down on the floor. Hard. She even pouted.

"TV and computer are my *life!*" Chloe wailed.

Her parents exchanged a look.

"That," said her mom, "is exactly the problem."

2

Seeing Red

Chloe lay on her bed clutching the petals of her bright pink, daisy-shaped bed cushion. She'd been sent to her room to cool down after yelling and stomping her foot. But she was far from being cool. Her face still felt red hot.

Chloe dug her fingers deeper into the pillow. It was her favourite piece from her official Maddie Mariposa bedding set. Not only did the daisy pillow look exactly like the one Maddie had in her bedroom on the TV show, it was good for squeezing when she was upset, too. Chloe was mad at her parents for their awful new rule. She pressed her fingers into the pillow so hard, her knuckles turned white. But it didn't help.

Chloe tossed her pillow against her bedroom wall, sending a few pictures drifting to the floor. Nearly the whole wall behind her desk was plastered with glossy pictures of Jake and Josh Taylor and Maddie Mariposa. Last year, Dylan Hardy posters had covered the wall. But ever since Dylan started going out with Yasmine Price, who played the snobby zombie on *Zoned Out*, he was no longer Chloe's all-time favourite TV star. Down came Dylan Hardy and up went Jake and Josh and Maddie. Hardly a single sliver of white paint showed through. Chloe had ripped some of the pictures out of magazines and bought the bigger posters with her birthday money. She proudly called it "Chloe's Wall of Fame." Mark liked to tease her and call it "Chloe's Wall of Lame." But what did Mark know, anyway? These were her favourite stars in the world. And now she wouldn't get to see what any of them were up to for a whole month!

"Urgh!" Chloe growled. She turned restlessly on her bed, the springs squeaking in protest. She could still feel the heat of her burning red cheeks and her red blood pumping in her tight fists. *Red. Red. RED.* She remembered her mom explaining the expression to her once. When someone was "seeing red," it meant that they were very angry. Thinking about how she couldn't watch TV or play games on the computer for a whole month, Chloe understood exactly what "seeing red" meant.

Red was the colour of Chloe's hot, angry face.

Red was the colour of *being* angry.

Mixed up with her feelings, even the white ceiling above her bed seemed red. Thinking about how there would be no more TV or computer for a whole month, she just couldn't get "red" out of her head.

Suddenly, Chloe swung her legs over the side of her bed and jumped onto the floor. She stomped over to her desk and yanked open the middle drawer. She grabbed a big piece of drawing paper and slammed it on her desk.

Next, Chloe pulled the lid off the old blue cookie tin where she kept her markers. She hunted until she found exactly what she wanted

— a big fat red marker. She tore off the cap. Pressing hard, she began to draw a small red spiral in the middle of the paper.

As she made the red spiral bigger and bigger, Chloe thought about how unfair her mom and dad were being. How come parents always got to decide what kids could and couldn't do? She drew another spiral on top of the first one. Then another and another. Each spiral became bigger and scribblier. *Red. Red. RED*.

How come her parents could say "let's do an experiment!" and all of a sudden Chloe would be the only one in grade four who didn't know about the coolest computer games or the latest songs from *The Taylor Twins*? She jerked the tip of the marker back into the middle of the page. She darkened the centre of the tangle of scribbly spirals with another layer of red.

Chloe stopped colouring when she realized that she was about to make a hole in her paper with the force of her scribbles. She leaned back in her chair, pushed a few stray curls out of her eyes, and took a good look at what she'd done. Her scribble kind of looked like a monster. A red, angry monster with hundreds of arms shaking angry fists.

As Chloe admired the red scribble-monster, she noticed something else. Her feelings inside didn't seem quite as red as they had before. It was like some of her mood had drained onto the paper. Chloe thought for a minute, a new idea coming into her head. Actually, a new colour.

Orange, Chloe thought. *Now I'm seeing orange.* Still hot. Still fiery. But not quite red.

She plunged her hand into the blue cookie tin again, this time pulling out an orange marker. She began to draw softer orange lines around the angry red fists.

3

The Chicken Dance

Chloe's family sat around the kitchen table. The only sounds were the *tick-tock* of the kitchen clock and the scraping of cutlery on plates.

Nobody said a word.

Chloe could feel the red and orange mood all around the table. All because of the unfair rule her parents had announced before supper.

Chloe had eaten half of her dinner and finished a whole glass of milk before her mom started talking. "Are we cooled down yet?" she asked, looking across the table at Chloe and Mark.

Chloe shrugged her shoulders. Mark just grunted through his perma-frown.

"I guess that will have to do. Your dad and I want to finish our talk about turning off the TV and computer for a month." Their mom gave them a warning look. "A *grown-up* talk."

Mark made a "whatever" kind of face. Chloe looked down at her plate. She used her fork to stir a couple of grains of rice around in a pool of reddish sauce. She was shaping them into a rice and sauce anger monster.

"We all watch way too much TV and spend far too much time with our computers — hours and hours and hours," their mom continued. "Your dad and I included."

Chloe looked up from her plate in surprise. "You mean you're going to follow the rule, too?"

Chloe's dad nodded. "That's right. No TV and no computer for all of us," he said. "I spend all day on the computer. At work, I don't have a choice." Chloe's dad was an engineer who worked for the City of Winnipeg. His job was to help design bridges and roads, and he used his computer a lot. "When I come home I do have a choice. This month, I'm going to choose to do hobbies that I like."

"But what about looking up vacations?" Chloe asked. Her dad liked to look up prices and deals for exciting vacations on the computer. Chloe had always thought that was weird since her family didn't go on many vacations. But Chloe's dad said he found it relaxing to just think about the places they might visit. "I thought that was your favourite hobby," she said.

"I do enjoy looking up trips. But it still means that I'm staring at a computer screen. I need to take a break."

Chloe crossed her arms. *Just because you need a break from the computer doesn't mean I have to take one too*, she thought.

"It's going to be a challenge for all of us," said her mom. "I'm not going to even look at my laptop once I get home from work."

Now that, Chloe thought, *is hard to believe!* Chloe's mom worked for the advertising department of the phone company. At home, she always seemed to have her laptop with her, to check her email and catch up on extra work. She even worked on her computer while she watched TV.

"And no more TV for your dad and me this month."

"Even *Legal Team: Seattle?*" Chloe asked. She knew that her parents loved that show as much as she loved *The Taylor Twins*. Chloe wasn't allowed to watch it because sometimes it showed gross stuff. Not that Chloe wanted to watch it, anyway. She couldn't stand the sight of blood. Even fake TV blood.

"That's right. No more *Legal Team: Seattle*."

"Where did you get this great idea, anyway — from *Valerie?*" Mark said, rolling his eyes. Their mom watched or recorded *The Valerie Nickel Show* every day. Valerie interviewed experts about stuff like exercising, cooking, fashion, and organizing your house. Their mom was always trying out lots of ideas from the show.

"Actually, yes. I did see something about this topic on *Valerie*," she said.

"That's ironic," Mark grumbled.

"What does ironic mean?" Chloe asked.

Chloe's dad looked thoughtful and rubbed his bristly hair. "Ironic is when what you say and what you do kind of go against each other. In a sort of funny way."

Huh? Chloe raised her eyebrow. She still didn't get it.

"Like Mom getting the idea to turn off our TV for a month *from* TV!" Mark said.

Chloe thought it over. "That *is* ironic, Mom!" she said.

"It's still a good idea," her mom said, narrowing her eyes. "Even if it came from TV."

"So TV isn't so bad," Chloe said. "That proves it!"

Her dad sighed. "We aren't saying that TV is bad. It's just that too much of it — too much of anything, really — can make you forget about what's important."

"Valerie interviewed a family that did this exact experiment," Chloe's mom explained. "They unplugged their TVs, computers, video games — everything. Except they did it for three months, not just one."

Chloe's jaw dropped. There was no way she would survive three whole months.

"At the end of the three months, the whole family said that they were much happier. They discovered all sorts of hobbies they'd forgotten about, or never knew they enjoyed. They spent more time together —"

"And they danced and held hands and lived happily ever after!" Mark said sarcastically.

"I'm going to do more cooking this month," said their dad, ignoring Mark. "I have a whole collection of great cookbooks, but I hardly ever take the time to try new recipes. This month we're going to have gourmet meals every day!" he declared.

Chloe thought *that* sounded good, at least. "No more leftovers?" she asked, poking at the remains of her sweet and sour pork on her plate. It had also been yesterday's supper.

"How about *fewer* leftovers," her mom said.

"And the leftovers will be so delicious, that you won't mind them at all," added her dad.

"I'm going to start taking kickboxing at the gym," Chloe's mom said. She bent her elbows and flexed her arm muscles.

Mark practically spit up his milk. Chloe's eyes widened. Kickboxing? Her *mom?*

"What's so strange about that?" their mom asked innocently.

Mark gulped his milk down. "Kickboxing is kind of . . . for jocks," he said.

Their mom shrugged. "So, what's your point? I played sports in high school and university."

Mark and Chloe exchanged a glance. "But, you're not a jock," Chloe said. "You're a *mom.*"

"Anyway, there's a class that starts this weekend, and I'm going to go," their mom said. "Lots of moms are a part of it. Jordan's mom is joining, too." Jordan Karsnicki was Mark's best friend from school. "She's the one who told me about it, actually." Chloe tried to picture her mom and Mrs. Karsnicki dressed in karate outfits, jumping through the air, shouting and kicking their legs. *The no TV and no computer rule is already making us crazy*, Chloe thought. *And we just started!*

"What are you two going to do with all of your spare time?" their dad asked, looking at Chloe and Mark.

"Probably sleep," Mark said.

"You're going to sleep every day after school until the end of June?" Chloe asked.

Mark shrugged. "Maybe."

"How about you, Chloe? What are you going to do?" her mom asked.

Chloe didn't say anything and concentrated on scowling. She was still in her orange mood — not quite red, but still mad at the rule. Secretly, she thought that she might make some more drawings like her angry red monster picture, but she didn't say that out loud. She wanted to make sure her parents knew exactly how unfair they were being.

"I'm sure you two will come up with some great ideas," their dad said. He pushed back his chair and started to clear the supper dishes while their mom went to the pantry, pulled out a box of cookies, and arranged a few on a plate.

"What happens if we break the rule?" Chloe asked. She reached for a chocolate fudge cookie.

"We hope that you follow our rule because it's the right thing to do," said her dad. "But I suppose it can't hurt to have some kind of a penalty." He looked at Chloe's mom. "What do you think, Michelle? A few dollars off their allowance per offence?"

"Nice going, Chloe," mumbled Mark through a mouthful of cookie crumbs. Chloe gave him a little kick under the table.

"That sounds fair to me. Let's say two dollars off your allowance each time you break the rule," her mom said. "But we won't have to worry about that, right?" she added.

"What about school stuff?" Mark said. "I have to use the computer sometimes for homework. Unless . . ." His face suddenly lit up. "I *could* tell my teacher that I'm not allowed to use the computer at home, and then —"

"No way," said their dad. "You're not getting out of homework. You and Chloe are allowed to use the computer *only* when it's for school."

"What about you guys?" Chloe said to her parents. "What happens if you break the rule?"

"We can't take away your allowance," said Mark. "That's not fair!"

Their parents exchanged a look. Their dad cleared his throat and said, "Well, I don't think that it's going to be a problem, so . . ."

"Uh-uh. No way," said Mark. "You need to have a penalty, too."

All of a sudden an idea came into Chloe's head. It was something that she had seen on *My Two Crazy Lives*, when Maddie tried to help her mom stick to her new diet. It was silly, goofy, and ridiculous — the perfect penalty for her parents.

"I know," she said with a slow smile. "If Mom or Dad break the rule, they have to do the chicken dance for three whole minutes." Exactly what Maddie made her mom do every time she got caught sneaking a chocolate bar. Chloe crossed her arms and added: "On the front lawn." TV *did* have some good ideas!

Their parents smiled. "Agreed," their dad said. "But you can get that picture out of your heads right now." He looked at Chloe, who had started giggling, and Mark, whose perma-frown was twitching. "It's not going to happen."

Chloe tucked her hands under her armpits and

flapped her arms like chicken wings. She laughed as she pictured her mom and dad standing on the grass flapping their arms and wiggling their hips as their neighbours walked by.

"*Bock-bock-bock!*" Mark clucked, joining in.

Soon, all four of them were laughing. Chloe liked laughing at jokes with her family, even if they made up unfair rules.

Yellow, Chloe thought, suddenly picturing the colour of sunshine in her head. *Laughing is yellow*.

4

Mr. Z's Garden

"I can help out a lot more with your flowers this month," said Chloe to her neighbour, Mr. Zilinski, a few days later after school. They were standing in his front yard by the flower beds.

Mr. Z shuffled over to his wheelbarrow, taking small, careful steps. He was the oldest person Chloe knew, and moved very slowly. "That's good news," Mr. Z said. He looked at Chloe from underneath the brim of his floppy sun hat, a friendly smile on his round, wrinkled face. "Do you want to help right now?" He reached into the wheelbarrow where he kept his gardening supplies and pulled out a small pair of green gardening gloves. They were the gloves that

Chloe wore whenever she helped take care of the flowers.

"Sure," said Chloe, reaching for the gloves. "But it's actually not good news. The reason I have more time is because my parents aren't letting us watch TV or play computer games for a whole month. Today is day four." She was crossing off each horrible day on her Taylor Twins calendar with an angry red "X."

"Is that right?" Mr. Z said. He crouched down near a cluster of cheerful orange flowers, which Chloe knew were called zinnias.

She could hear Mr. Z's knees creak as he lowered himself down and gently pinched off a few dead leaves from the tall, straight stems.

Mr. Z was very old and lived next door with his gentle, brown and white dog, Ozzy, and his cat, Lewis. Chloe's family helped Mr. Z with little jobs around his house and yard. Mark shovelled his walkway in the winter and mowed his grass in the summer. Her mom and dad watered his indoor plants and took in his mail whenever he went to Vancouver to visit his daughter, Sharon, and his granddaughter, Amanda. Chloe helped him water and weed his flower beds and planters in the summer, usually on the weekends.

Chloe liked helping Mr. Z. She learned the names of lots of different flowers. The red ones were geraniums. The purple and yellow ones were pansies. The sunny golden-coloured ones with the dark centres were called black-eyed Susans. Chloe also loved Ozzy and Ozzy loved her, too. He stuck to Chloe like glue when she worked in the garden, hoping for some pats or a belly rub.

As much as she liked helping out, Chloe couldn't stop thinking about missing her all-time favourite after-school TV show. *I'll bet Jake and Josh are singing their brand new song today, and I can't watch!*

"It's not fair," Chloe complained out loud. "I can't watch my shows or play my games. Not even *Interstellar Jellyfish Invasion.*" She fell onto her knees and began untangling weeds from pink flowers called impatiens.

"Hmm," said Mr. Z.

"How come adults get to make all the rules?" Chloe gave a good yank to a stubborn weed. "Just because *they* decide to do something doesn't mean they should force their kids to do it, too."

"Hmm," Mr. Z said again.

The two worked in silence for a while, pulling out weeds, snipping dead leaves, and pinching off dried out blooms. A bee buzzed in the air, and Ozzy made snuffling noises with his big wet nose as he poked around under Mr. Z's shrubs. Even though Chloe was upset, and kept thinking about how unfair her life was, she remembered to be very careful when pulling up weeds. Mr. Z had shown her how they like to grab on tight to the flowers. You had to take care to pull out the bad stuff and leave the good stuff alone.

"When I was your age," Mr. Z said as he watered the big clay flowerpot full of orange begonias with his green watering can, "we didn't have a TV."

Chloe stopped her weeding and sat up straight. As soon as she did, Ozzy leaned in closer to her. He knew that when her hands weren't busy with the weeds, she could give him pats.

"Really?" Chloe said. She took off one of her gloves and stroked Ozzy's fur. "Were you poor?"

"Well, we weren't rich," Mr. Z said. He put down the watering can and reached behind his back as he straightened up. Chloe thought he looked sore. "But we weren't exactly poor. Believe it or not, TVs weren't even invented when I was a boy."

Chloe's jaw dropped. Mr. Z must be *ancient!* She didn't say it out loud, though, knowing that it might sound rude.

"What did you do for fun?" Chloe asked, trying to imagine life without even one TV. The Lamberts had three TVs in their house! Lots of Chloe's friends even had their very own TV in their bedroom.

"Oh, we did many, many things," said Mr. Z, smiling. "I liked playing ball in the summer and climbing trees. My little brother and I used to pretend that we were soldiers."

Chloe tried to picture Mr. Z as a little boy. All

she could imagine was a little-boy body with the wrinkled, old man face that he had today.

"But what about at night before bed and stuff? Wasn't it boring without a TV?" Chloe asked.

"I guess we didn't know what we were missing, so we didn't think about it that way. And we did have the radio."

Chloe raised her eyebrows. *The radio?*

"When I was a boy, they used to broadcast exciting plays on the radio. My whole family would gather around to listen. Kind of like how your family might watch a show on TV."

"But there weren't any pictures!" Chloe said, confused. It was hard to imagine how a play on the radio could be exciting.

"Oh, we didn't need pictures. All we had to do was listen, and we could see the story in our heads." Mr. Z looked up, as though he were remembering. "There were the sounds of slamming doors, thunder, and gunshots. And of course, there was music — sad or romantic, funny or scary. It depended on the story."

Chloe thought about her family sitting around

a radio listening to a story. That might be kind of cool. Of course, Mark would probably roll his eyes and say it was for babies. But Mr. Z had been a boy once, like Mark, and he thought the radio was fun.

Suddenly, a surprising idea occurred to Chloe about Mr. Z.

"Do you have a TV *now?*" she asked. Maybe he didn't! Chloe had never seen a TV in his house. Of course, although she spent a lot of time in Mr. Z's flower garden in the summer, she hadn't been inside his house very often. Chloe was allergic to cat hair, and Mr. Z's fat orange housecat Lewis was very hairy. She couldn't be in the same room as a cat without having a million sneezes.

But Mr. Z chuckled. "I have a TV. In fact, I have two. One in the living room and one in my bedroom. TV keeps me company sometimes."

"Do you have a computer?" Chloe asked. She was pretty sure he would say no. Her Gran and Pa didn't have one, and they weren't as old as Mr. Z. Gran said she was worried someone would steal money from them over the Internet. Chloe thought that was pretty silly, but maybe Mr. Z felt the same way.

But her neighbour surprised her. "I use my computer every day to email my granddaughter. It's cheaper than the phone!"

"Oh," Chloe said. Not every old person was scared of computers after all.

Chloe and Mr. Z went back to their weeding and watering. Chloe tried again to picture Mr. Z as a little boy without wrinkles or creaky knees or a hearing aid, but it was too hard. Instead, she tried imagining herself as a grown-up. She had long, smooth, straight hair like Maddie Mariposa. Chloe thought about what her house might look like in the future and the kind of things she might have in it that hadn't been invented yet.

"Chloe," Mr. Z said, interrupting her day-dream. "Should I leave the geraniums for you?"

"Thanks, but you can do them if you want," Chloe said.

"All right," said Mr. Z. He snapped off some of the geranium stems with the withered red blooms. "I seem to remember that the geraniums are your all-time favourite flowers. You always take care of them best."

"Oh," Chloe said. "That was last summer. The hydrangeas are actually my favourites now."

"I see," Mr. Z said, looking at Chloe, a smile crinkling the corners of his eyes.

Chloe walked over to the tall, beautiful white hydrangeas. They had big green leaves and huge white blooms shaped like globes that were almost the size of Chloe's head.

"When I grow up and have my own house, my flower garden will only have hydrangeas," Chloe declared. She pictured herself, her long Maddie Mariposa hair flowing in the breeze, standing between clusters and clusters of white hydrangeas.

"Hmm," said Mr. Z. "That might be very nice, Chloe. All that white and green. As for me, I like having all kinds of flowers in my garden."

"But which flower is your favourite?" Chloe asked.

Mr. Z rubbed his back. He looked thoughtful.

"Well, in the early spring I love tulips. I like how they open up in the morning and then close up tight at night. And later in the spring, the black-eyed Susans look so cheerful, as long as the rabbits don't eat them up, of course!"

"But you can only have one favourite at a time," Chloe insisted.

"Hmm," he said with a smile. "Maybe yes, maybe no."

Even though Mr. Z couldn't figure out which flower he liked best, Chloe certainly knew her all-time favourite.

As Chloe pulled out a tall, skinny weed, a great idea came into her head. She didn't have to wait for her future house. She could have all the hydrangeas she wanted, right now! She would make them herself. Chloe thought of how she could shape the full, white blooms out of pieces of tissue tied together with string. And she remembered seeing a box of pipe cleaners in the basement. She could twist a few of the green ones together to make the long stems.

Besides, what else was Chloe going to do

tonight, anyway? It's wasn't as though she could watch her TV shows or play computer games.

5

Conspiracy!

"Hello!" Chloe shouted, dropping her school bag onto the floor in the front hall. No one answered.

It was a grey, rainy Thursday after school, too wet to help out in Mr. Z's garden. *Where is everyone?* Chloe thought, kicking off her wet shoes. Usually her mom got home before she did.

"HEL-LOOO!" Chloe called again. Still nothing.

Mark is home, she thought, eyeing his muddy, size-twelve runners. Then she spotted the yellow sticky note on the door of the front hall closet:

> Dad and I will be back
> around six Mark is in
> charge Love Mom

41

"MARK!" Chloe shouted. Still no answer. She climbed the stairs that led to the bedrooms. She noticed Mark's door was open just a crack. Muffled voices floated into the hall. She peeked through the crack . . .

There was Mark, sitting on his unmade bed. Chloe could tell that he had headphones tucked into his ears beneath his messy mop of hair. Not only that, the headphones were attached to the video game he held in his hands. He was pressing buttons at lightning speed and shouting "Gotcha!" every now and then.

"You're not allowed to play that!" Chloe shouted, ignoring the skull-and-crossbones "Enter at Own Risk" sign that hung on his door.

Mark jumped off his bed, ripped his headphones out of his ears, and whipped the game behind his back. His face was red.

"I saw that!" Chloe said, rushing over to the bed. "You were playing your game. That's breaking the rule."

"What are you going to do, tell on me?" Mark said. He was trying to act cool, but Chloe could tell from the quiver in his voice that he was nervous.

"Why shouldn't I tell?" Chloe asked.

"So I broke Mom and Dad's rule," Mark said. "Big deal! It was just this one time. I was bored."

Chloe placed her hands on her hips. "It's not fair if you get to break the rule. I bet you'd tell on me if I was the one who was on the computer!" Chloe said. She spun around on her heels, turned up her nose, and walked to the door. It wasn't often that she got the better of her older brother, and she was going to make the most of it.

"Chloe, wait," Mark said. "Don't tell! I have a better idea."

Chloe stopped and turned around. "What?"

"How about," Mark said slowly, "if I let you watch a bit of TV?"

Chloe furrowed her eyebrows. "But then we'd both be in trouble."

"No, dim-wit. Mom and Dad won't be home until six o'clock. You can watch one of your dumb shows until five-thirty and no one would ever know."

"They're not dumb shows, and I'm not a dim-wit. Take that back!" Chloe said. But she was thinking about Mark's idea. If Mark wasn't going to tell on her, she could watch *My Two Crazy Lives*. Sasha told Chloe they were going to replay the very first episode of the series today. Chloe had never seen it before. It explained how Maddie Mariposa discovered her secret talent for fashion design. It started in five minutes . . .

"Fine, you're not a dim-wit, and your shows aren't dumb," Mark admitted with a sigh. "So what do you say? You watch your show, I play a bit more of my game, and we both agree not to say anything to Mom and Dad."

Chloe wasn't sure. Part of her knew that she shouldn't break the rule, even if her mom and dad would never find out. That part of her wanted to say "no way!" to Mark and stomp out of the room. But the other part of her really, *really* wanted to see the first episode ever of *My Two Crazy Lives*.

"It will only be this one time," Mark said, as if reading her mind. "Then we'll go back to keeping the rule the rest of the month."

Chloe didn't say anything for a moment. She was thinking. Her parents would never know she had watched her show if she and Mark didn't tell. And was it really a lie if you just didn't say? And what if they never showed the first episode of *My Two Crazy Lives* on TV ever again . . .

"Okay," Chloe decided. "Just this once."

Mark nodded, gave Chloe a thumbs-up, and stuck his headphones back in his ears.

Chloe headed downstairs to the family room. Her heart was beating fast, and her hands felt kind of clammy, just like the time she had accidentally put a hole in one of her dad's big old-fashioned speakers with a soccer ball. She hadn't even done anything wrong yet and she was already feeling guilty.

She marched down the two steps that led into the family room and grabbed the remote control, determined to go through with it. Her heart was pounding, and her face felt red. It wasn't the same as the "angry red" feeling she had the other day, when her parents first announced their unfair new rule. As she stood there facing the blank TV,

Chloe felt more like a whole bunch of colours had been jumbled together inside of her. Not in a pretty way like a rainbow. Instead, it was like someone had dumped a whole set of paints and smeared them all together into a muddy, brownish mess.

Should I turn it on, or not? Chloe thought.

On the one hand, she didn't want to disappoint her parents. And she'd done really well for the last seven days (she was still keeping track of the days on her calendar). She hadn't thought of turning on the TV and had even avoided standing near the computer in the kitchen so she didn't have to think of the games she was missing.

On the other hand, Chloe still asked Sasha every day at school what had happened on their favourite shows the night before. Her parents hadn't said that she couldn't *talk* about TV with her friends.

But talking about it isn't the same as watching, Chloe thought. And if Sasha was right and they were actually going to play the first episode of *My Two Crazy Lives*, the one she had never seen . . .

I'll just check and see if it is the first episode, Chloe decided. *If not, I'll shut it off.*

Chloe clicked the red "On" button on the remote control. *Zap.* The theme song of *My Two Crazy Lives* had just begun:

When this world tries to get you down,
And turns your smile right into a frown,
Just remember your secret, your talent inside
Remember that you have two crazy lives!

The show started. Chloe knew instantly that she had seen this episode before. It was the one where Maddie secretly designs clothes for the school fashion show, but snobby Selena Delaney takes all the credit. It wasn't the first episode ever of *My Two Crazy Lives.*

But it sure is a good one, Chloe thought, her heart still pounding. She kept watching.

During the first few minutes of the show, she kept turning her head to listen for the sound of the front door opening, expecting her parents to show up at any moment. Her insides still felt mixed and muddled. She wasn't having very much fun.

CRASH!

Chloe jumped in her seat. What was that? It took her a moment to realize that the noise had come from upstairs. *Mark*, Chloe thought. He was probably leaping around his room like he always did when he was really into his game. Chloe relaxed a little. She watched a commercial about Maddie Mariposa's new jewellery-making kit. *Maybe I'll ask for that for Christmas*, Chloe thought, sinking deeper into the couch.

Suddenly, a noise came from the front entrance of the house. Chloe could hear someone jiggling a key in the doorknob. This time it really was her mom and dad!

"Hello!" they called as they walked through the door.

Chloe sprang from the couch. She looked around frantically for the remote control. It had been beside her a second ago — but where was it now? Her heart was thundering in her chest.

Her parents were taking off their shoes and

raincoats. Maybe they couldn't hear the TV . . .

"Hello!" Chloe shouted. "How was your day? You're home early. Did you bring supper?" She hoped that her voice would drown out *My Two Crazy Lives*. Aha! The top of the remote control was sticking out from between the couch cushions. Chloe grabbed it and zapped off the TV. She sat down on the couch and tried to look casual.

Her mom walked into the family room. "How was school, Chloe?" she asked, looking at her quizzically. Chloe watched her mom's gaze fall on the remote control on the cushion beside her.

"Were you watching TV?" she asked.

Her dad joined them in the family room.

Chloe looked up at her parents. Her throat felt very dry. She felt as though she couldn't speak.

"What were you doing in here, Chloe?" her dad asked. "I don't see any of your books or drawings."

Chloe opened her mouth to respond. She was thinking of saying, "I was just sitting in here thinking," but she knew that it would be useless. She knew that the awful muddy brown feeling that had swelled up in her chest again wouldn't go away if she did that. It would just get muddier.

"I was watching *My Two Crazy Lives*," she said, lowering her eyes.

Her mom let out a disappointed sigh. "Oh, Chloe," she said. "You were doing so well."

Chloe was quiet.

"Where's Mark?" her dad asked.

"In his room," Chloe said. Her dad headed out of the room and straight for the stairs.

She wondered if Mark was still playing his game or if he had heard his parents come in and had hidden it in time. *I'll bet I'm the only one who's going to get in trouble*, Chloe thought miserably.

But a minute later, Mark and her dad came down the stairs and into the family room. Mark was still holding his game. He'd been busted, too.

"All right," said their mom, hands on her hips. "What's the story? Out with it."

"I just turned on my game to see what level I got to last week," Mark mumbled, staring at his feet. "Jordan asked me today, and I couldn't remember."

Their mom shook her head. Their dad raised his eyebrows. They didn't look impressed. "You said that you wouldn't use that thing," their mom said, gesturing toward the game in Mark's hand. "You told us we could trust you and that we didn't have to take it away."

"But Jordan told me about this trick to beat the falling boulders. I tried it, and then I . . . just kept playing."

"Chloe," said their mom. "Why did you turn on the TV?"

Chloe gulped. She looked at Mark, and Mark looked back at her. For half a second, she thought about blaming him, saying it was all his idea. But that wasn't really true.

"I wanted to see the first episode of *My Two Crazy Lives*. I've never seen it. Sasha said it was on today."

Their dad shook his head. "I think it's a funny coincidence that you both decided you would break the rule today." He said "funny" in a way that meant he thought it was just the opposite. "Is there more to the story here?"

Finally, Mark admitted: "I told Chloe she could watch TV."

"Why?"

"Because she caught me playing my game. I told her she could watch TV if she didn't tell."

"So," said their dad with a low whistle. "There was a conspiracy on top of breaking the rules."

"What's a *conspiracy?*" Chloe dared to ask.

"A conspiracy is when people pull off a crime together and then agree to cover up for each other," said their mom.

Sounds like something from Legal Team: Seattle, Chloe thought. But she didn't say it out loud.

"You know this means you'll both be losing money from your allowance. And you can hand over that game right now, Mark," their mom said, stretching out her hand. Mark gave her the video game, with the frowniest of perma-frowns. "I'm especially upset about the sneaking and the covering up."

"I think that this incident cancels the whole

week of good behaviour. Especially the conspiracy," said their dad. "What do you say, Michelle? Should we tack on another week?"

"Sounds fair to me," said their mom.

Not to me! Chloe thought. Mark's jaw dropped. An extra week without TV or the computer? At this rate, Maddie Mariposa would be a grandma before Chloe ever got to watch her show again!

Chloe didn't feel muddy brown anymore. She felt grey, like a gloomy day.

6

Charades

"What are we going to do tonight?" Chloe called out to her dad, who was cooking in the kitchen. She hoped that his latest gourmet dish would actually turn out. Last night he had tried making butter chicken. It was supposed to be the same recipe the Lamberts loved from The Gardens of India restaurant. Instead, it tasted like an old shoe covered in ketchup. Chloe made a face as she remembered.

Chloe was kneeling at the coffee table in the family room, hunched over her latest drawing. She had a purple pencil crayon in her hand and was putting the finishing touches on a rainbow. When she was finished, Chloe was going to hang her picture on the wall behind her, with some of the other drawings she had made that week. Chloe liked how her drawings made the family room look like an art gallery.

It was Saturday, day nine of the rule on Chloe's calendar. Saturday was almost always family movie night at her house, before "The Rule," of course. They would rent two movies — one chosen by Chloe, the other by Mark. They would order a large deluxe pizza from their favourite pizza place and settle in front of the TV for the night. Later, they might pop a big bag of microwave popcorn.

"I'm making a new recipe for dinner — Enchiladas Supreme Casserole," Chloe's dad called over the *clink-clank* of the pots and pans and the classic rock that was blaring out of the radio. Her parents had agreed that listening to music was allowed, as long as you were doing something constructive while you were listening.

Chloe's dad loved old rock music, and he had a whole collection of records that had belonged to *his* dad when he was a teenager. He had shown a few of the records to Chloe. She liked the colourful, swirling, weird drawings on the big square record covers. Whoever made them must have had a lot of imagination. Her dad told her they were works of art.

"We're not ordering from Pizza NOW! tonight?" Chloe asked, disappointed. She hoped that pizza wasn't the next thing on her mom and dad's list to be banned. Although she had to admit there were some delicious smells coming from the kitchen.

"You're going to love this recipe," Chloe's dad said. "I'm putting on extra cheese, just for you." Chloe's stomach growled. She adored gooey, melted cheese.

Chloe leaned back and admired her rainbow. Earlier that day, she had gone over to Sasha's house to play in the sprinkler. When she held her hand over the tall shafts of water, a colourful, misty rainbow appeared, and her picture looked just like it. She admired how she had drawn the water spraying out in all different directions. She had also done a pretty good job of drawing the shimmering red, orange, blue, and green colours and had even glued silver sequins on the page to be shiny water drops, glittering like diamonds in the sun.

Chloe stood up with her picture and turned around to face the wall behind the couch, where her artwork was hanging. In the centre of the wall was the scribbly, red, angry monster. She loved how the bold colour leapt right out of the white wall. She called it *Chloe's Wrath* after asking her dad what another good word for "anger" was. To the left of *Chloe's Wrath* was something she called *Laughter*. Chloe imagined that laughter was like sunshiny, yellow bubbles that danced and floated and bounced. She had cut circles out of yellow paper in different sizes and arranged them on the wall in a special pattern to make it look like there were bubbles floating up from the ground. Chloe had hung some other colourful paintings and drawings on the wall, and had decorated the room with a few of her white tissue paper hydrangeas. It really did look like an art gallery!

As Chloe was deciding exactly where in her "gallery" to hang her latest creation, her mom walked into the family room through the back door. She was still dressed for kickboxing class.

"Hey, guys!" she said.

"Hi, Michelle," Chloe's dad called back from the kitchen.

"Hi, Mom," Chloe said, looking up from her drawing. Her mom's hair was pulled back in a very messy ponytail and her face looked hot and kind of sweaty.

"How was it?" Chloe asked.

"It was fun," her mom said enthusiastically. "Check out this new move!" She made fists with her hands and held them up near her face. For a moment, she stood very still. Then, all of a sudden, her right leg shot out and up, and she gave the air a vicious kick. She made a sound like *"Huh!"* Chloe jumped back, even though her mom's foot was nowhere near her.

"Pretty cool, eh?" her mom said, returning to a normal standing position.

Chloe nodded.

"That looks really pretty, Chloe," her mom said, noticing Chloe's new picture. "Is that a rainbow?"

Chloe nodded. "I saw it when I was playing in the sprinkler with Sasha."

Her mom looked closely at the drawing. "Are those water drops?" she asked, pointing to the sparkling sequins.

"Yes." It felt good when someone knew right away what the things in her drawing were. "Can you help me hang it up?" Chloe asked.

She and her mom put some sticky putty on the back of her drawing. Her mom pressed the big piece of paper next to *Chloe's Wrath*.

"What are we going to do after supper, since we can't watch movies?" Chloe asked.

"We've spent the whole day doing our own things," her mom said, wiping her sweaty forehead with the back of her hand. "I think it would be nice to have some family time."

"But what will we do?"

"Oh, I don't know. Maybe we could have a board game tournament. Or make a puzzle. Or . . ." her mom's face lit up. "We could play charades."

"What's charades?" Chloe asked.

"You've never played before?"

59

Chloe shook her head.

"It's one of my favourites from when I was a girl. We played it at camp," her mom said. "You'll love it!"

* * *

Chloe wasn't so sure she loved charades.

Her parents explained the game to her and her brother. Each person had to think of an object, or something like the title of a book or a movie. Without telling anyone else, they had to write their ideas down on a piece of paper and put it in their pocket. Then, without talking or pointing to things, they had to act out whatever they had written on the paper.

Charades *might* have been fun if it hadn't been for Mark. Everyone was trying to have a good time, except him. He kept rolling his eyes and complaining about how boring the game was, especially when it was Chloe's turn. She would barely start to act out her idea, when Mark would guess it and she'd have to sit right down.

Where was the fun in that?

"My turn," said Chloe's dad.

Chloe stomped back to the couch and dropped into her seat, a gloomy look on her face. Mark had just guessed "window" about three seconds into her turn. Of course, he had been right. Why couldn't she think of anything harder? *Charades stinks*, Chloe thought.

Chloe's dad scribbled his idea on a piece of paper and folded it up. He cracked his knuckles and did a few neck stretches. He looked like he was about to jump onto the hockey rink rather than take a turn at charades.

Mark groaned. "Are we almost finished?"

"Be a sport, Mark," their mom said. "There are worse ways to spend a Saturday night."

"I doubt it," Mark mumbled.

"Oh, I don't know," their dad said. "The upstairs bathroom could use a good cleaning."

"Or there's your bedroom closet. You've been promising to organize it for the last two months," said their mom.

"Okay, okay. I'll play," Mark said.

"You'll be glad you did," said their dad. "You wouldn't want to miss this one!" He smiled mysteriously.

Chloe could barely believe what happened next. Her dad began to do a strange dance, swaying his body this way and that, making rippling motions with his arms over his head. Chloe was sure glad that she hadn't invited Sasha over. This was embarrassing!

"What are you supposed to be, Rick?" her mom asked, biting her lip and trying not to laugh. "A belly dancer?"

Chloe thought her mom might burst. Mark, on the other hand, looked horror-stricken at his dad's wacky dance. Chloe thought it was pretty embarrassing, too. Although, it was also kind of funny . . .

Suddenly, still swaying and waving his arms around, he puckered up his mouth, and then opened it very wide. He did this again and again, looking kind of like . . .

"A fish!" Chloe guessed.

"A bird!" her mom called out.

"A weirdo," Mark muttered.

But Chloe's dad shook his head. He moved closer to the couch where Chloe, her mom, and Mark were sitting, still doing his crazy dance and making that strange fish mouth. He leaned so close to Chloe that she could have pinched his nose.

All of a sudden, her mom let out a huge whoop of laughter. It wasn't the soft kind of laugh Chloe sometimes heard her mom use on the phone when she was talking to a client from work. This was a big, happy, silly kind of laugh. She tried to talk but could barely catch her breath. She even snorted a couple of times.

"What . . . in . . . world . . . supposed . . . be?" Chloe's mom gasped.

Not only did her dad look ridiculous, Chloe thought her mom looked funny too, with her purple face and all those snorting noises coming from her nose. Soon Chloe was laughing, too. She had to hold her stomach, which was quickly beginning to ache from her giggles.

"You guys are all nuts," said Mark, trying to be

cool. But Chloe saw her brother's perma-frown was twitching. Their dad must have noticed too, because he moved closer to Mark's face with his fish mouth. Suddenly, Mark's messy hair began to shake. Next, his perma-frown disappeared. Finally, he burst out laughing harder than everyone else! Mark had the same kind of snorting laugh as their mom, only louder.

Their dad tumbled onto the couch beside Mark. The four of them sat there, squished like sardines, giggling and snorting. Mark's laughs turned into hiccups. For some reason, this seemed hilarious to everyone, and they all laughed even louder.

When they finally calmed down, Chloe asked, "So what were you supposed to be, Dad?"

"You really can't guess?" her dad asked. Everyone shook their heads, with the occasional snort escaping.

"I was a lava lamp!"

Chloe's mom whooped again.

"You mean like the one on the bookshelf?" Chloe asked with a giggle, looking at her dad's weird old lamp. He had brought it up from the basement with his old records. It looked like a glass rocket and had coloured liquid inside. When you plugged it in, the coloured stuff formed into bubbles and floated around. Chloe's dad said that people who listened to classic rock liked lava lamps.

"I was being the bubbles." Her dad started doing his dance again. Chloe thought that the funniest part was the fish face.

"Okay!" Chloe's dad said with a clap of his hands. "Who's next?"

7

Busted!

"Mom!" Chloe called out. She raced upstairs to her mom's bedroom. It was Monday, just after school. Chloe was holding a painting she had made of a gigantic tortoise. Her class had gone on a field trip to the Assiniboine Park Zoo in the morning. They had to make a picture of their favourite animal in Art that afternoon. Chloe's teacher, Madam Wilson, said that hers was very artistic.

Chloe stopped at the top of the stairs when she heard a strange noise. It sounded like a whole squad of police cars was driving down the street. She peered over the railing and out the large windows at the front of the house. She couldn't *see* any police cars . . .

She listened more closely and realized that the noises weren't coming from outside — they were coming from one of the bedrooms. "Mark!" she said under her breath and marched toward his room. He must be playing a video game with a car chase! Chloe wondered how he had the guts after being caught last time. Not only that, he knew that Mom was home. *Boy, is he going to get it!* Chloe thought.

But just as she was about to knock on Mark's door, he came out of the bathroom at the end of the hall.

"Stay away from my room!" Mark said, with a grunt.

"But I thought . . ." Chloe started.

Another siren wailed. Mark heard it too, and looked at Chloe. "That sounds like it's coming from . . ."

They raced toward their parents' bedroom. Mark threw open the door.

Sure enough, there was their mom, sitting on the edge of her bed — watching TV! Chloe and Mark stared at her, their mouths hanging open.

Their mom's face turned beet red. She leapt up from the bed, snapped off the television, and faced her children.

"Mom, you are so BUSTED!" Mark said with a gleeful grin.

"You're right, you're right," their mom said, holding up her hands in surrender.

"You broke your own rule!" Chloe said incredulously.

Her mom, face still bright red, said, "It was a really tough day at work. I was just about to change out of my work clothes and relax on the bed with a book."

Chloe noticed that her mom's white blouse was only partly tucked into her grey skirt, and that she was still wearing one of her high-heeled shoes. A big book sat unopened on the bed.

"I looked at the clock and thought 'Hmm . . . *Legal Team: Seattle* is on right now.' And then . . ."

"And *then* . . ." Mark prompted with a stern voice.

"*And then* . . . I turned on the TV," their mom said, hanging her head.

The three of them were quiet for a moment. Then Mark said, "I think we should get the allowance money back that you took from us."

Their mom shook her head. "No way. I shouldn't have watched TV today, but what you and Chloe did the other day was still wrong."

Mark sulked.

Chloe shook her head in disappointment at her mom. Ever since charades night, she had been thinking about how much fun she and her family were having not watching TV or playing on the computer. *How could she break her own rule?*

"You have to do the chicken dance," Chloe said firmly.

Her mom smiled. "Oh, Chloe. I won't watch any more TV. I promise. It was a momentary lapse."

"On the front lawn," Chloe insisted.

"We were just being silly when we decided about that," said her mom, a hint of panic in her voice. She looked at Mark for support. But he crossed his arms and shook his head.

"*I* wasn't being silly," said Chloe. "And you

and Dad agreed." She crossed her arms too and stared at her mom.

"She's right," Mark said. "We all agreed. We'd lose our allowance for breaking the rule, and you and Dad would have to do the chicken dance."

Their mom was quiet. Finally, she let out a sigh. "Okay," she said. "Let's get this over with."

Chloe marched out of the bedroom and down the stairs. Mark followed, snickering loudly. Their mom was last, walking slowly on purpose.

Chloe kept marching right through the front door to the middle of the lawn. Mark stood beside her. They pointed to a spot in front of them.

Their mom took her position and looked to the left and to the right. She gave her hips a little wiggle, and then quickly said: "Okay, I think that's enough."

Chloe said, "No way!"

Mark tapped his watch. "Three minutes. And you have to dance like you mean it before you're off the hook."

"Flap those arms!" Chloe shouted.

Their mom sighed heavily. "All right," she said, and began to dance like a chicken. This time, she flapped her arms like wings and wiggled and twisted, sticking her backside out behind her. Chloe and Mark began to laugh hysterically.

Their mom jutted her chin in and out, like a chicken grazing for food, and took chicken steps back and forth around the lawn.

Chloe and Mark howled.

"Am I almost done?" their mom asked, still wagging her neck back and forth like a hen. "I want to go *bock*, *bock*, *bock* to the house!"

Chloe clutched her stomach.

"*Forty . . . more . . . seconds!*" Mark said through snorts.

Their mom was still being a chicken when Chloe heard a door squeak open nearby.

"Hi, Mr. Z!" she called to her neighbour. He was standing with Ozzy in his front doorway.

He raised his hand in the air. "Hello there, neighbours! Having fun?" he called, looking quizzically at Chloe's mom.

Chloe looked over at her mom. Her face was as red as Mr. Z's geraniums.

8

A Ghost in the Radio

"Did you ever play charades with your family?" Chloe asked Mr. Z. She was pulling up stray dandelions that had sprouted up near the hydrangeas. Ozzy was investigating the pile of weeds beside her.

"Hmm," Mr. Z said. He was on his knees hunched over one of his flowerpots, turning the soil with a little spade. "No, I don't think so."

"My family plays it every Saturday night now," Chloe said. "It's really funny. It's my all-time favourite game."

"Hmm," Mr. Z said again. "I thought you had a different favourite game. What was it, now . . . *Space Jellyfish Attack?*"

"You mean *Interstellar Jellyfish Invasion*," Chloe corrected him. "That's a computer game. I'm not allowed to play those, remember?"

"That's right, of course." Mr. Z nodded his head. "I'm an old man, you see. Sometimes things get loose up here and I forget." He chuckled as he tapped the top of his floppy sun hat with his muddy, garden-gloved finger. Chloe giggled.

"Anyway," Chloe said. "Charades is *much* better than *Interstellar Jellyfish Invasion* and *Swamp Creature Showdown*, and all my games combined! It's definitely my all-time favourite."

"It sounds like your family has lots of fun on Saturdays," said Mr. Z, once again bending over his flowerpot.

"We do!" Chloe said enthusiastically. "Once my dad did this funny dance, and we all laughed so hard we almost cried. He was a lava lamp. And last Saturday Mark thought he was going to fool me, as usual. But it only took me *three seconds* to figure out that he was a telescope. It was lots of fun!"

Chloe thought some more about Saturday-night charades. "I don't think we ever laughed as hard during movie night," she said, half to herself. "Did your family listen to funny plays on the radio before you had TV?" Chloe asked.

Mr. Z straightened up slowly. "I do remember listening to some comedy shows. But my favourite radio shows were the scary ones. In fact," he said, looking around as though he thought someone might be listening, "just thinking about them still gives me the shivers. Even after all these years."

Chloe's eyes widened. But then she scrunched up her face and tilted her head to one side. "Is that true?" she asked. She could understand how a scary *movie* could give you nightmares. She hated seeing blood and guts. But if you couldn't *see* the gross stuff, it couldn't be that scary, could it?

"There was one story that I will never, ever forget." Mr. Z leaned forward and spoke in a hushed voice, as though he were telling a big secret. "It was called *The Ghost Walks at Midnight*. On dark, stormy nights, I have nightmares about it to this day."

"Why was it so scary?" Chloe asked, a lump rising in her throat. Ozzy trotted closer to her and nuzzled against her side. Maybe he could tell that she was a little bit scared by Mr. Z's strange, quiet voice.

"There was a little girl in the story, just about your age, who found herself spending the night all alone in a big, old mansion. Everyone thought the house was haunted, but the girl wanted to show her friends just how brave she was."

"What happened?" Chloe asked quietly, squeezing closer to Ozzy's soft, warm body.

"Around midnight, just as the little girl was about to drift off to sleep, she heard the door to her room creaking open. Creeeeeeeaaaaaak!"

Chloe was leaning forward, wondering what would happen next, when . . .

"GOTCHA!" Mr. Z shouted suddenly.

"Eek!" Chloe screeched, sending a handful of dandelions into the air. Ozzy let out a howl.

But then she saw that Mr. Z was smiling. His wrinkles shook as he laughed. Soon she was giggling, too. She patted Ozzy so that he wouldn't be afraid. His tail started to wag.

"Kind of scary, eh?" Mr. Z said.

Chloe nodded.

"And just think — you and I are sitting outside in the sunshine on a bright summer day. Imagine listening to such a story with your family on a cold, windy winter's night."

Chloe's heart was still thumping hard. "Did you and your family always have so much fun together?"

"Hmm," said Mr. Z. "We did have some wonderful times. I remember my dad played ball with us. Mother could tell even scarier stories than the ones we heard on the radio. And of course," he grinned, "my brother and I were a couple of little troublemakers, always getting into scrapes."

Chloe thought about Mr. Z listening to scary stories on the radio with his family, and getting into mischief with his brother. She thought of how much fun her family had on Saturday night eating the enchilada casserole or her dad's new homemade everything-on-it pizzas (*much* better than Pizza NOW!), playing charades, and doing things together instead of separately in front of a screen. An idea was beginning to take shape in her mind. "I bet the whole world was better off before TVs and computers . . ." she murmured.

"Hmm," said Mr. Z. He went back to turning the soil in the flowerpot. "Maybe yes, maybe no. It wasn't all fun and games when I was a little boy, Chloe."

"What do you mean?" Chloe asked.

"Well, for one thing, it was the Depression."

Chloe knitted her eyebrows together. "What's the Depression?"

"It was when people didn't have much money, and it was hard to find a job. My dad was lucky. He had a job, but he had to work long, hard hours. He'd leave first thing in the morning and wouldn't be home until I was tucked into bed." Mr. Z looked up as he remembered. "And Mother — her job never stopped. She was always cooking and cleaning and sewing and taking care of us, all without the fancy machines we have today. And children back then," Mr. Z looked right at Chloe, "didn't have all the books and tools and computers that you have for learning. In fact, some children had to get a job instead of an education, so they could help support their families."

Chloe thought about what Mr. Z said, trying to imagine how different things were way, way back then. The Depression didn't sound like fun at all. "But still," she said, "even though it was hard, you had fun when you listened to the radio together and did all sorts of other things as a family. You didn't need any TVs or computers."

"Hmm," was all Mr. Z said. He looked like he was still remembering.

"Maybe everyone should shut off their TVs and computers," Chloe said. The idea in her head was getting bigger and bigger.

Mr. Z patted the soil neatly into place in the pot. "Maybe yes, maybe no."

9

Double Busted

Chloe ran down the stairs toward the kitchen, her latest drawing flapping in her hand. It was called *Radio Ghost*. She had used pastels to draw a creepy ghost floating out of an old-fashioned radio, like the one at her Gran and Pa's cabin. Mr. Z's scary story had given her the idea.

"Dad!" she shouted. "Do you have any extra recipe cards? I want to make labels for the drawings in my art gallery. Then maybe . . ." Chloe didn't finish her sentence. She was too surprised at what she saw when she turned the corner into the kitchen.

Her parents were standing in front of the family computer with guilty looks on their faces.

Behind them, Chloe could clearly see that the computer was on. In fact, a video was blazing across the screen, and a voice drifted out of the speakers. *"Be sure to lower the heat before adding the vegetables . . ."* said the voice.

"What are you doing?" Chloe asked. She couldn't believe it! Her parents were using the computer. They were BOTH breaking the rule, right in front of her!

"Well, uh . . ." her dad said. He looked down at the floor.

"Sauté until the onions are a light, golden colour . . ." continued the voice. Chloe's mom reached over and clicked the mouse to shut off the video.

"How could you break the rule?" Chloe said indignantly. "Even Mark and I haven't played computer or watched TV or anything since that one time!" Chloe couldn't get over it. Sure, this was the first time her dad was guilty. But her mom had already danced like a chicken on the lawn. Of all people, she should know better!

Her dad looked at her mom, and then at

Chloe. He puffed out his cheeks, and exhaled.

"You're right, Chloe. You guys have been ter-
rific, and we messed up. *Mea Culpa*."

Mea Culpa? "What does that mean?" Chloe
asked.

"It means 'my fault.' You caught us."

"But why did you do it?"

Her dad sighed. "I was trying to make tradi-
tional *Osso Bucco* for dinner. It's supposed to be
wonderful — braised veal shanks, tender vegetables, served with a yummy risotto and . . ." he
said, with a glint in his eye, the one he got whenever he talked about a new gourmet dish. Chloe
raised her eyebrows at him, unimpressed.

"Anyway," he said, "my recipe wasn't working
out. I have a feeling my cookbook missed a step
or two. So I went online to find some tips to save
our dinner."

Chloe *did* notice a funny smell coming from
the kitchen, kind of like burnt garbage. She had
never tried *Osso Bucco* before but was pretty sure
it shouldn't smell like garbage. Not that burnt
Osso Bucco gave her dad an excuse for using the

82

computer. The Lamberts were still supposed to be offline for another ten days!

"When your dad told me what he was doing on the computer," Chloe's mom continued the story, "I remembered this great cooking site that has all sorts of video demonstrations. That's what we were looking at."

"A-*ha!*" Chloe said dramatically. "It was a conspiracy!"

Her parents exchanged a glance. "Well, maybe not quite a conspiracy," said her mom.

"And we *were* trying to save dinner . . ." her dad said, a pleading look in his eyes.

But Chloe shook her head. "You still need to do the chicken dance on the lawn. Both of you."

Her dad looked hesitant.

"Come on, Rick. It's not so bad," said her mom, grabbing her husband by the arm.

"But, the *Osso Bucco!*" Chloe's dad said desperately.

"The *Osso Bucco* bit the dust. It's Pizza NOW! tonight," said Chloe's mom.

"And no more TV or computer, you guys,"

said Chloe, "or I might have to come up with another penalty. Something even worse than the chicken dance!"

"I can't imagine what that could possibly be," muttered her dad. "All right! Let's get this over with before Mark gets home. If he sees me dancing around the yard, I'll never hear the end of it."

As if on cue, Mark strolled into the kitchen. He sniffed at the air, his nose wrinkling in faint disgust. He looked at Chloe, then at his shamefaced parents.

"What?" he said. "Did I miss something?"

"No," said Chloe, a little smile forming at the corners of her mouth. "You got here just in time . . ."

10

The Picture-Perfect Day

"Lights out!" Chloe's dad called from the top of the stairs.

Chloe, dressed in her pyjamas, looked up from the picture she was drawing and at the clock beside her bed. How did it get so late? It felt as though she had just started drawing.

"Five more minutes?" Chloe called back. She heard a soft tap at her door. Her dad pushed it open gently and stuck his head in the room.

"I'm just finishing up," Chloe said.

"What are you working on now?" her dad asked. He stepped into the room and stood behind Chloe, who was sitting at her desk, and looked over her shoulder.

"It's a picture of today at the park," she said. She adjusted the reading lamp so that her dad could get a better look.

"That looks great," he said. "Very creative."

Chloe smiled. She was really proud of this one. Not only was it a great drawing, but it also reminded her of a great day. Maybe the most perfect day she'd ever had.

Chloe had divided a huge piece of paper into four squares. In each square, she drew a memory from the day with her family at Kildonan Park, a large city park near her house. It was full of enormous trees, rolling hills, creeks, flowers, and fields. In the winter, her family would sometimes go there to skate on the pond or sled down the slippery toboggan runs. But for some reason, they hadn't ever spent much time there in the summer. After today, she wondered why they didn't go to Kildonan Park every day. It was definitely her new all-time favourite place.

"This is me on my bike," Chloe said, pointing to the first square.

She had drawn herself on her purple bike

soaring down a tall hill. The Red River was on her left, a canopy of trees soaring high over her head. She drew her hair sticking out from under her blue helmet and lines swooping back from her clothes, making her look like a blur as she hurdled down, down, down. The picture made Chloe feel the gust of air that her bike had created and the butterflies in her stomach as she stopped pedalling and just let her bike tires spin.

"And this must be the four of us at the Witch's Hut," said her dad, looking at the second square in Chloe's drawing.

The Witch's Hut was a little cottage tucked away in the trees in the middle of the park. It was from the story of Hansel and Gretel. They could actually go inside and see a scene right out of the fairy tale. The cottage was dark and damp. Chloe thought that it smelled a bit like railroad tracks on a hot day. Inside, there was a statue of poor little Hansel locked away in a cage. When they climbed the staircase to the second floor, they found Gretel holding a broom and taking orders from the terrible witch herself! Chloe had drawn her family members with nervous faces looking at the witch. She made sure that the witch looked as ugly in her drawing as she had looked in the cottage, with mean eyes, a big crooked nose, and a huge black wart growing on her chin.

The third square in the picture showed Chloe twirling and looking up at the sky. Instead of drawing lines going straight back, like she had done to show speed on her bike, she drew circles of colours around her body, to make it look like she was really spinning.

"What are these blurry colours over your head?" her dad asked, pointing to the green and gold cloud above Chloe's twirling body.

"That's how the leaves on the trees looked when I got dizzy from twirling," Chloe said.

In the last square was a picture of the barbecue supper that the Lamberts ate before heading home. Chloe drew her dad grilling hot dogs over a fire pit. Her mom and Mark had set up a net nearby and were playing badminton. Chloe was patting a little black Labrador puppy named Lexie, who had walked by their picnic spot with her owner. The sun was just starting to set in the sky, turning it pink, purple, and gold. Chloe had used pastels for the sunset so that she could make the different colours fade into each other, just like it had looked in real life. It was her favourite part of her picture.

"You've sure enjoyed drawing lately," her dad said. "How would you like to take art lessons this summer at the art gallery?"

Chloe's face lit up. "Really?"

"I saw a poster at the library advertising classes for kids your age."

"Is the art gallery that building that looks like a big wedge of cheese?" Chloe asked.

"That's the one," said her dad.

Chloe had been to the Winnipeg Art Gallery last year with her grade three class. They had gone to look at paintings about nature. The building itself was made out of grey stone and was shaped like an enormous triangle. One side was the skinny part of the triangle, and the rest of the building got fatter and fatter. Chloe remembered her teacher, Monsieur Sabourin, telling the class that if you looked very carefully at the stone walls, you could find ancient fossils. She and Sasha had searched for fossils together and found seventeen different ones.

"That sounds fun!" Chloe said.

"All right. I'll sign you up on Monday. But now it's time for bed." Her dad kissed her on the top of her head and walked toward the door.

"Okay," said Chloe. She took one more look at her best drawing yet and snapped off her desk lamp.

She crawled under her covers thinking about her family's perfect Sunday at the park. She drifted to sleep with thoughts of bike rides and Hansel and Gretel and ancient fossils in her head.

11

No More Machines!

"Do you know something?" Chloe asked her dad and Mark at breakfast the next morning.

"Yeah, I know something," said Mark. "I know that two plus two is four, and that we breathe oxygen, and that we're human beings, and —"

"Mark!" said their dad, standing at the kitchen counter, buttering a piece of toast.

"That's not what I mean," Chloe said, scowling across the table at her brother. "Do you know something, *Dad?*" Chloe said again, purposely ignoring Mark. "Yesterday at Kildonan Park, we didn't use a single machine!"

"Is that right?" her dad said. He took a big slurp of coffee.

"We went on the swings, and played bad-minton. You even cooked our supper over a fire. You see? No machines!"

"That's very interesting, Chloe."

Chloe nodded. "We're not watching TV or using the computer anymore, and we're having more fun. No one's even been busted for a week!"

"Even Mom," Mark mumbled, gulping his orange juice.

"And the day we had the *most* fun of all," Chloe continued, "we didn't use a single machine!"

Mark snickered as he slurped his cereal. "Are you saying that we should never use any kind of machine again?"

"Maybe I am," Chloe said, with a toss of her head. "Maybe things would be more fun all the time."

Mark laughed sarcastically. "Yeah, right."

"You like it when we play charades, right?" Chloe said.

"It's all right."

"See? You admit it!" Chloe said, her voice

getting loud. "And you had a good time at the park, without machines. I saw you laughing and everything!" She insisted. Mark just shrugged and kept slurping and crunching.

"Did you know that Mr. Z next door lived before there were any TVs or computers? He tells me stories about the fun he and his family had listening to scary stories on the radio, and playing ball together, and all sorts of stuff." Chloe's voice was still rising. "So that proves it! Machines aren't any fun at all." She pounded her fist on the table. Mark's orange juice glass jumped.

"Oh, yeah?" Mark said, looking up from his cereal, a challenge in his eyes. "What do you call the thing we drove in to get to the park?" he said. "A car is a machine. The way I see it: no car, no park, no fun."

"Urgh!" Chloe growled. Why was her brother so annoying? "But when we got to the park —"

"Yeah, yeah," Mark interrupted. "I'd like to see you try and live without machines. You wouldn't last a day."

Chloe narrowed her eyes. As she looked at Mark, she started to feel red inside, like her angry monster. He always thought he was so great. She'd show *him!*

"Fine!" Chloe said. "I won't use any more machines. And it will be fun — you'll see!"

"Good luck," Mark muttered, clearly not meaning it at all.

"What do you want for breakfast, Chloe?" her dad asked. "Toast or cereal?"

Chloe thought for a moment, and then said: "Cereal, please. No milk." Her dad handed her a bowl of cereal without any milk.

"What's up with that?" Mark grunted, eyeing Chloe as she nibbled on her dry cereal.

Chloe looked straight at her brother. "Milk comes from the refrigerator, which is a machine. So I'm eating cereal without milk." Chloe scowled at the refrigerator.

"You're weird," Mark said. "Besides, how do you think that cereal was made?"

Chloe stopped nibbling and looked down at her bowl.

"Your cereal was made by a machine," Mark taunted. "And it was put into the *box* by another machine. Oh — and the box was made by a machine. And then it was sent to the store by a truck, which, in case you were wondering . . . *is a machine!*"

"Fine, I get it!" Chloe said miserably. She had to eat *something*. "I can't help it how things were made. I'm just not going to use any *more* machines." She turned her face away from her brother.

Mark got up, his chair squeaking on the floor. "Like I said, you won't last a day."

"I will too!" Chloe said. When she finished eating her cereal, Chloe asked her dad if she could walk to school instead of taking the bus.

"Not unless you go back in time and start walking a half an hour ago," her dad said. "It's too far, and you'll be late."

"Can I ride my bike, then?" Chloe asked. A bike wasn't really a machine, was it? It didn't use gas like a car, and you didn't have to plug it in.

"No," her dad said. His "no" sounded very

final. "Now get ready or you'll miss the bus."

Chloe went upstairs to the bathroom to wash her face and brush her teeth. But she didn't flick on the lightswitch. After all, lights needed electricity and electricity came from a machine. Chloe did her best to get ready in the dark. She spilled the toothpaste on the counter twice because she couldn't see her toothbrush very well. And her face felt a bit sticky from some soap she had left on her face by mistake, but she was going to show Mark that she could do it. No more machines!

Maybe her dad would let her walk to school tomorrow if she got up really early. Today was only the first day of her "No Machines" life. She would just have to do the best she could.

On the school bus, Chloe sat with Sasha and told her about her new plan.

"But I thought you hated your parents' rule," Sasha said suspiciously, twirling a blonde curl around her finger. "Why would you make it even worse for yourself?"

"I didn't know any better before," Chloe

explained. "But we have all sorts of fun now without machines. I bet you can't even imagine."

"Not really," said Sasha. "How come all of a sudden you think all machines are so bad?"

"TVs and computers are machines, and life is more fun without them. So I've decided not to use any more machines."

Sasha raised her eyebrow. "Is this like the time you said you weren't going to wear pink *ever again* because the Taylor Twins said they hated that colour?"

"That was different," Chloe said, looking down at her bright pink t-shirt. "Besides, who needs the Taylor Twins, anyway?"

"Since when don't you like the Taylor Twins?" Sasha asked. "Last week, you told me that you wanted to *marry* Josh Taylor. You said, 'He's my all-time favourite.'"

"Shhh!" Chloe looked around, embarrassed. "He's not anymore! I don't want to have anything to do with the Taylor Twins or TV, or any machine again unless I totally, absolutely have to!"

Sasha didn't look convinced. "You're wearing

a watch," she said, pointing to Chloe's wrist. "That's a machine."

Chloe looked down. Without a word, she unfastened her watch's bright yellow strap and shoved it in the front pocket of her school bag. "There," she said, zipping up the pocket.

Sasha just shook her head.

At school, Chloe did her best not to use any machines. There wasn't much she could do about the lights in her classroom, or when Madam Wilson showed the class a short movie about volcanoes (although Chloe did try to keep her eyes shut most of the time). And every time Chloe felt the urge to look up at the clock on the wall — another machine — she stopped herself with a little shake of her head, the same as Ozzy did when he got water in his ears.

When it was time for activity stations, Chloe chose reading first instead of computer. When it was time for her reading group to use the computers, Chloe asked Madam Wilson if she could do art instead. Her teacher said it was okay, since she had finished all her computer work and it was almost the end of the year. Chloe sat alone at the craft table and made badges out of blue paper that said *NO MORE MACHINES!* in bright yellow letters. She stuck one to her t-shirt with tape and tried to get all her friends to wear them.

"You'll have a lot more fun without machines," Chloe kept promising everyone. Most of the kids in her class looked at her like she was crazy. But Chloe didn't care. She knew she was right. A couple of girls wore Chloe's badges, although Chloe didn't think they really understood. Even Sasha just rolled her eyes as she stuck the badge Chloe made for her onto her shirt.

By lunchtime, Chloe was feeling quite proud of herself. She had done pretty well avoiding machines so far. *So there, Mark!* she thought. Suddenly, she noticed a yummy smell filling the air. She had forgotten — it was hot dog day at school, her all-time favourite! Chloe's stomach growled and her mouth started to water. Pretty soon the volunteer parents would come to her classroom with hot dogs and chips and fruit juice. In fact, her mom, who had the day off from work, was supposed to be helping cook the hot dogs in the school kitchen. She always tried to be one of the parents who delivered the hot lunch so that she could say hi. Chloe was wondering if she would see her mom, when suddenly it hit her — she couldn't eat hot dogs anymore! Hot dogs were cooked on a stove, and the stove was a machine! *I guess I'll just have to starve*, she said to herself in misery. Her stomach growled even louder.

The lunch bell rang. A couple of parents arrived at the door to the classroom pushing a cart stacked high with hot dogs. Chloe's mom was one of them. Jason Rosner's dad was calling out the names, and Chloe's mom was handing out the food.

"Chloe Lambert," Jason's dad said when he got to the "L" names.

Chloe pushed back her chair and walked up to her mom.

"Hi, Chloe! Here's your lunch."

Chloe looked at the foil wrapper around the juicy, mouth-watering hot dog. "I'm not hungry." Her stomach growled so loud that she was sure everyone in the class could hear it.

"Are you feeling sick, hon?" her mom asked.

"It's not that," she said. "I'm not eating any-thing that was cooked with a machine."

Her mom raised her eyebrows. "Chloe, you have to eat." She held out the hot dog.

Chloe took the bag of potato chips. "I'll eat these," she said. She was going to take the fruit juice, too, but remembered that it had been in the fridge.

"Fine," her mom said. "You don't have to eat any of this, but you do have to take it. I don't have room to keep it on the cart." Her mom gave Chloe a look that said: *We'll talk about this at home.* Chloe reluctantly took her hot dog, drink, and chips and went back to her desk.

Jason's dad called out the rest of the names. Chloe sat at her desk, staring at her food. She tried as hard as she could not to look at her friends eat-ing their lunches, or to smell the delicious scent of hot dogs in the air. She opened up her bag of potato chips and bit into one of her chips.

Crunch.

Chloe reminded herself that life without machines was supposed to be fun. But when she looked over at Sasha giggling with some of the other girls as they munched on their tasty hot dogs, she knew that it was hopeless. She couldn't miss out, even if it had taken a thousand machines to get this hot dog into her hands.

She pulled back the wrapping and took a huge bite. It was perfect and yummy and had lots of mustard, just the way she liked it.

12

Where's Mr. Z?

Chloe got off the bus at her stop with Sasha. She noticed that Sasha wasn't wearing her *NO MORE MACHINES!* badge anymore. Chloe was still wearing hers, but the shoulder strap of her school bag had crushed it. It was crumpled and torn, just like Chloe's feelings. Ever since she bit into the hot dog at lunch, she realized that it was impossible to live without machines, even for a day. Of course, the worst part about it was that Mark was right!

Chloe waved goodbye to her best friend and slowly began the short walk to her house. She dragged her feet, imagining Mark waiting for her at home so that he could tease her about her failure. She ripped off her badge and shoved it in her pocket. She decided that she would stop in first at Mr. Z's to ask him if he needed help in his garden. *That might cheer me up*, she thought. Plus, she wouldn't have to face Mark right away.

Chloe arrived at the little walkway that led to Mr. Z's front door. But something was wrong. Where was Ozzy? He always sat in the front yard on a sunny day, waiting for Chloe to come home from school and give him pats and a belly rub. But he wasn't there.

Chloe also noticed a strange car in the driveway. She knew Mr. Z didn't drive anymore because of his bad eyesight, so it didn't belong to him. She couldn't remember him ever having company over. Whose car could it be?

She wasn't sure why, but she suddenly felt worried. She ran to her house, forgetting all about her *NO MORE MACHINES!* badges and Mark and getting teased. She would ask her mom or dad. Maybe they knew what was going on with her friend.

Chloe pushed open the door to her house and

dropped her school bag with a loud *thud* on the floor. She was about to call out to her mom when she spotted her sitting on the couch in the family room talking on the phone. Her mom held up her hand, signalling for Chloe to be quiet. She had a serious look on her face.

"Oh, yes. I see, Sharon," she was saying into the phone. "We appreciate the call. I'm sorry for Victor, but it's good that you and Amanda are here."

Victor — that's Mr. Z's name! Chloe thought. Amanda was the name of his granddaughter from Vancouver. What was going on?

"Let us know if there is anything we can do. Thanks, Sharon." Chloe's mom hung up the phone. As soon as she did, Chloe started asking questions.

"Were you talking about Mr. Z? Is he okay? Where's Ozzy?" Chloe felt her heart flutter.

"Mr. Z is in the hospital," her mom said. "He had to have an operation. That was his daughter, Sharon, on the phone."

"An operation!" Chloe said, her eyes wide.

"But he wasn't even sick!" She was breathing fast.

"You're right. On the outside, Mr. Z didn't look sick," her mom said. "But Sharon told me that his doctor found a problem inside, with his heart. Nobody could see the problem except with a special test."

"Why didn't he tell us?" Chloe felt her lip quiver. She hated even thinking of operations. "Is he . . . going to be . . . okay?" Chloe could barely get the words out. She remembered watching a movie once where a person was having an operation. There wasn't any blood of course, or Chloe could never have looked. But there was a machine beside the operating table that went *beep! beep! beep!* to the beat of the patient's heart. In the movie, the beeps got slower and longer until they just went *beeeeeeeeeeeeeep*, meaning that the patient's heart had stopped. *What if that happened to Mr. Z?*

Chloe's mom patted the cushion beside her on the couch. Chloe sat down. Her mom reached out and brushed Chloe's curls away from her face. Usually, Chloe didn't like it when her mom did

106

that. But right then she didn't mind.

"Sharon said that the operation went very well. Mr. Z is going to need lots of rest, but his doctor thinks he's going to be fine."

Chloe leaned against her mom's shoulder.

"Did he need lots of stitches?" Chloe asked, wincing. She thought that stitches were gross.

Her mom continued to stroke her hair. "He probably needed a few."

"Do they hurt?"

"Stitches can be uncomfortable. But the doctors are taking very good care of him." Her mom looked thoughtful. "It's pretty amazing what they did, actually."

"What do you mean?" Chloe asked.

"Sharon was explaining it all to me on the phone," her mom said. "She's a doctor, too."

Chloe nodded. Mr. Z had told her lots of times.

Her mom continued. "Mr. Z's heart wasn't beating properly. So his doctors put a tiny machine right inside his chest that will help it work again."

"A machine?" Chloe's eyes got wide. "Does it stay inside of him? Even after the operation?"

"Yes," said Chloe's mom. "It's called an implant. Sharon said that it will stay in there for the rest of his life to keep his heart strong."

"If . . . if he didn't have the machine inside him, would he . . . die?" Chloe asked, her voice a whisper.

"No one knows the future, hon. But Sharon said that it was very lucky they found the problem when they did. It sounds like Mr. Z would have been a very sick man without the operation."

"Is he all better now?" Chloe asked.

"He will need a good rest. He'll be in the hospital for a little longer, and then he'll come home and rest some more."

"Who's taking care of Ozzy and Lewis while he's in the hospital?"

"Sharon and Amanda are staying next door. They'll take care of the pets."

Chloe was quiet for a moment. She thought of how she tried to prove to Mark that machines were no good. She thought of the badges she had made for her friends. And now there was a teeny tiny machine inside Mr. Z, making his heart beat.

"You look like you're thinking," her mom said.

Chloe nodded. "Yeah." Suddenly, her argument with Mark seemed silly.

"Can we go and visit Mr. Z in the hospital?" Chloe asked.

"That sounds like a nice idea. You and I will go in a few days, after he has had some time to rest, okay?"

Chloe thought of Mr. Z lying in a hospital bed. She didn't think he would like that very much, especially when it was so beautiful outside. Chloe knew that he would miss his flowers.

Suddenly, she knew exactly what she was going to bring Mr. Z when she went to visit him.

13

Flowers for a Friend

Chloe and her mom stepped into the hospital elevator. Chloe, who was clutching a bulging green canvas bag, pushed the button for the fourth floor. Her palms were sweaty. She didn't like hospitals. They had a funny smell, and seeing so many people in wheelchairs made her feel sad. But she was glad that she was going to visit Mr. Z. Sharon had phoned them the day before to say that he was doing much better and would love a visit.

Chloe and her mom stepped out of the elevator when it reached the fourth floor. Her mom scanned the piece of paper in her hand. "Look for room 408," she told Chloe. They followed the winding hallway until they came to the right room. Chloe's mom knocked gently on the open door.

"Come in," said a lady's voice.

Chloe followed her mom into the room. There was a lady and a teenaged girl sitting by the hospital bed. The lady stood up and said hello. She was Mr. Z's daughter, Sharon. She introduced the teenager as her daughter, Amanda. Amanda had long, shiny brown hair and a friendly smile.

Chloe said hello, and then looked at the bed where Mr. Z was resting. At first, she didn't even recognize him. For one thing, he wasn't wearing his big, floppy gardening hat. She wasn't used to seeing his shiny, practically bald head. He looked smaller and skinnier than usual. And he had dark brown circles under his eyes that made him look tired.

But when he saw Chloe, and smiled at her, he looked a bit more like the Mr. Z that she knew.

"How are you feeling, Victor?" Chloe's mom asked. She walked over to the bed and touched Mr. Z's hand.

"Much better, Michelle. Thank you," he said with a tired smile. "I'm feeling slow and old again, just like normal!" He chuckled a little bit.

"Oh, Dad," Sharon said.

"Is it true that you have a tiny machine inside of you?" Chloe asked. It was still hard to believe.

Mr. Z nodded. "That's right. It gives my heart a little kick every time it decides to slow down!" He winked at her.

"Does it hurt?" she asked biting her lip.

"My stitches are a bit itchy, but inside I feel just fine. Are you sure they really put anything in there, Sharon?" He tapped his chest and looked at his daughter, his eyes smiling.

"Oh, Dad," she said again.

Chloe smiled at her friend. He was laughing and joking and didn't even seem to be hurting too much. He was going to be okay.

"What's in the bag, Chloe?" Mr. Z asked. "You look like Santa Claus!"

Chloe looked down at the bulgy green bag she held in her hands.

"I made something for you," she said. She put

the bag on the floor and reached in. She started to pull out a cardboard flowerpot filled with tissue paper flowers on pipe cleaner stems, but stopped. "I guess you already have a lot of real flowers," Chloe said, noticing the get-well bouquets on the windowsill by Mr. Z's bed. Maybe he wouldn't want her fake flowers.

"I may have some nice bouquets, but you're the first to bring me black-eyed Susans!" Mr. Z said, looking at the yellow tissue-paper flowers in the pot in Chloe's hands. Chloe smiled and put the pot on the table beside the bed. Mr. Z looked at them and beamed. "These are beautiful, Chloe. You're becoming quite the artist."

Chloe felt her cheeks turn pink. She had been thinking about becoming an artist one day, but hadn't told anyone else yet.

"I made a few more," she said, reaching back into the big bag. "I know that you have lots of favourite flowers."

"Only if you have the space for them, Victor," Chloe's mom said.

"Of course I do!" said Mr. Z. "It will be like

having my flower garden right here."

Chloe was glad. This was what she hoped he would say. She lifted a second cardboard pot out of the bag.

"Petunias!" Mr. Z said, looking at the pink flowers.

"And those," he said as she pulled out the last pot, "with the very straight stems and different colours . . . those must be zinnias."

"These are cool," said Amanda, taking the pots from Chloe and arranging them on the windowsill. Chloe felt proud.

"All I need now are Ozzy and Lewis, then this room would be just like home!" Mr. Z said, giving Chloe a great idea for her next art project.

"You'll be home soon enough, Dad," Sharon said.

"And we're taking good care of 'the boys,'" said Amanda, giving Chloe a wink. Chloe liked Amanda. She seemed nice.

"All right, Victor. We're going to let you get your rest," said Chloe's mom. She motioned to Chloe to pick up her bag.

"Leaving so soon?" he asked.

"You've got to rest so that you can come home soon," Chloe said.

"Will you help me with my flowers when I get back?" Mr. Z asked.

"Of course!"

"Then it's a deal."

14

Back Online

The first thing Chloe did when she and her mom got home from the hospital was to get out her biggest pieces of paper and her box of pencil crayons. She spread out her supplies on the kitchen table and got right to work. She had planned her newest art project on the car ride home. This one wouldn't hang in her art gallery in the family room. It would decorate the white walls in Mr. Z's hospital room.

There would be two drawings. One would look like a window, with Lewis the cat peeking out, just like he did when Mr. Z worked in his garden. The second picture would be a life-sized drawing of Ozzy. She would cut around the outline of Ozzy's shape. She was even going to glue brown patches of felt onto his coat so it looked more like real fur.

She was concentrating on colouring Lewis's fur just the right shade of orange with her pencil crayons, when her mom came in the room.

"Do you know what day it is?" she asked.

Chloe shrugged and took a guess. "Sunday?"

"It is Sunday. But it's also been exactly thirty days since we turned off the TV and the computer."

"Really?" Chloe asked, looking up from her drawing. When she had first started counting the days of the no TV and no computer rule on her calendar, the end seemed ages and ages away.

"I have a secret," said her mom, sitting down across from Chloe at the table. "I recorded the season finale of *The Taylor Twins* for you a few weeks ago. You can watch it whenever you want."

Chloe raised her eyebrows. "But don't Mark and I have an extra week to go, because of the time we broke the rule?" Chloe asked. Mark would probably give her a kick for reminding her mom about the extra week offline.

"We haven't forgotten about that. But your dad and I think that overall, you and Mark have done really well. Sometimes, even better than we did."

She smiled at Chloe. Chloe returned the grin, remembering how silly her parents had looked doing the chicken dance in the front yard.

"It wasn't such a bad month, was it?" said her mom.

Chloe shook her head. "We did lots of fun stuff."

Her mom smiled. "There's a whole long summer ahead of us. I'm sure we'll figure out lots more fun things to do." She pushed her chair back from the table. "Anyway, you can watch your show whenever you want, if you feel like it."

Chloe thought about it for a moment. It might be fun to watch *The Taylor Twins* again. Sasha said that Jake and Josh sang their best song ever on the season finale.

"I think I will later," Chloe said. "But first I'm going to finish these drawings for Mr. Z."